June Bug Jamboree

by
Robin Martin Duttmann

Illustrations by Kalpart

Strategic Book Publishing and Rights Co.

Strategic Book Publishing and Rights Co.
12620 FM 1960, Suite A4-507
Houston, TX 77065
www.sbpra.com

For information about special discounts for bulk purchases,
please contact Strategic Book Publishing and Rights Co. Special Sales,
at bookorder@sbpra.net.

ISBN: 978-1-62857-863-8

For Noah and Cici, I love you both so much.
For my past and present students, and coworkers,
at St. James School. And for my best girlfriends,
what would life be without friends to celebrate!
With Love, Robin

Sally Slug

Was cuttin' a rug

While the June Bug Band did play.

Grandpa Spider

Sat down beside her

And spoons began to play.

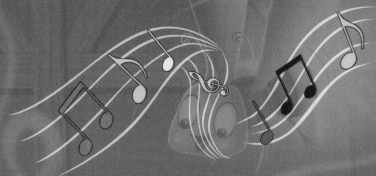

Fireflies glow

And do-si-do

To the music all night long.

A butterfly and an ant nearby

sing their favourite song.

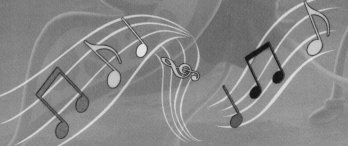

Twirl to your left,
Spin to your right,
We're gonna rock this place tonight.
Ho come fiddle,
Fiddle come fee,
Come and wiggle and dance with me,
At the June Bug Jamboree.

Deep fried chicken
Was finger lickin',
So was the pecan pie.

Moth did boast,
"I ate the most!"
So much he couldn't fly.

Potato bug

Drank a mug

Of the best moonshine there be.

He asked to dance

With the fancy ants;

There was one but he saw three.

Twirl to your left,
Spin to your right,
We're gonna rock this place tonight.
Ho come fiddle,
Fiddle come fee,
Laugh and giggle and dance with me,
At the June Bug Jamboree.

15

Caterpillar
Did the jitter
In her brand new shoes.

Willy Worm
Wiggled and squirmed
As he sang the blues.

Skip and bow,
Twirl the cow.
Oh, how we did dance.

Laughed and giggled,
Jiggled and wiggled,
'Till I split my pants.

Oh,

Twirl to your left,

Spin to your right,

We're gonna rock this place tonight.

Ho come fiddle,

Fiddle come fee,

Laugh and giggle and dance with me,

At the June Bug Jamboree.

22

CPSIA information can be obtained
at www.ICGtesting.com
Printed in the USA
LVIC06n2040071114
412586LV00001B/1